Take me out to the Ball game

Maryann Kovalski

Scholastic Canada Ltd.

Jenny and Joanna were baseball mad.
"Play ball!" they would call to anyone they could find.

Fly balls, grounders. Pitch, hit, slide. "You're out!"
Then, "One more game!" they'd shout.

Only one call could make a game stall
and Grandma's came one day —

6

"I'd like to know where you want to go?"
And snap! like that they sang . . .

Take me out to the ball game,

take me out to the crowd!

Buy me some peanuts and Cracker Jack,

I don't care if I never get back!

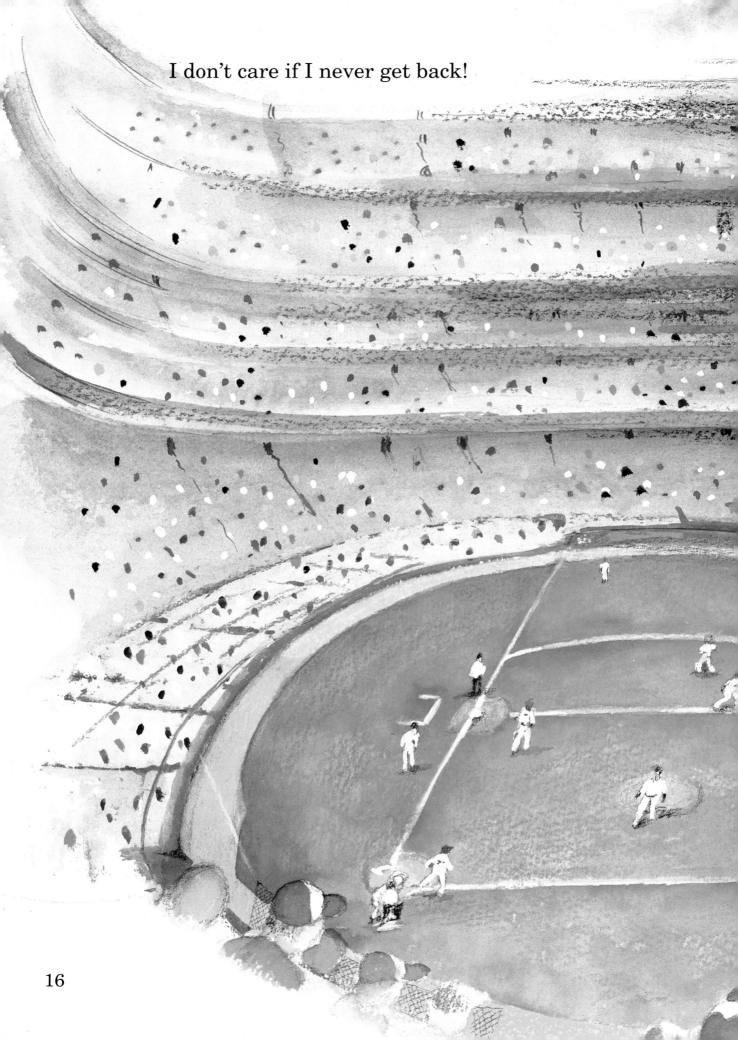

Let me root, root, root for the home team,

if they don't win it's a shame!

For it's one . . .

two . . .

three strikes —

"You're out!"

At the old ball game!

Take Me Out to the Ball Game

Words by Jack Norworth

Music by Albert von Tilzer

Take me out to the ball game,

Take me out to the crowd._____

Buy me some pea – nuts and crack – er jack

I don't care if I nev- er come back, Let me

root, root, root for the home team, If

they don't win it's a shame._____ For it's

one, two, three strikes, "You're out!" at the

old ball game. _____

For Gail

Scholastic Canada Ltd.
123 Newkirk Road, Richmond Hill, Ontario, Canada L4C 3G5

Scholastic Inc.
730 Broadway, New York, NY 10003, USA

Ashton Scholastic Pty Limited
PO Box 579, Gosford, NSW 2250, Australia

Ashton Scholastic Limited
Private Bag 1, Penrose, Auckland, New Zealand

Scholastic Publications Ltd.
Villiers House, Clarendon Avenue, Leamington Spa,
Warwickshire CV32 5PR, UK

6 5 4 3 2 1   Printed in Hong Kong   4 5 6 7/9

Canadian Cataloguing in Publication Data

Kovalski, Maryann
  Take me out to the ballgame

Includes musical score.
ISBN 0-590-74315-5

I. Title.

PS8571.093T3   jC813'.54   C93-094615-4
PZ7.K68Ta 1994